LUCY
TRIES
LUGE

written by

Lisa Bowes

illustrated by

James Hearne

ORCA BOOK PUBLISHERS

This is Lucy

and her brand-new luge sled.

It's shiny and strong and a bright shade of red.

It's a big day for Lucy.

She'll take her first ride

down a track that looks

like a wild tunnel slide!

But Lucy is nervous—
will her sled go too fast?

With such twists and turns,
she's afraid she might crash!

Lucy's dad says,
"Don't worry!"

Lucy's mom says,
"You'll be
great!"

Lucy decides to try.

Hurry!
Don't be
late!

Wearing a helmet for safety
and a race suit for speed,
Lucy runs to the start house.
Courage is all she needs!

She sits down on her sled
and takes a deep breath.
(Whew!)

The starter asks,
"Ready?"

Lucy answers,
"All set!"

The clock
starts to
tick down

3 2 1

At the sound of the

BEEP

Lucy's off on her run!

Pushing first with her hands,
Lucy lies on her back.

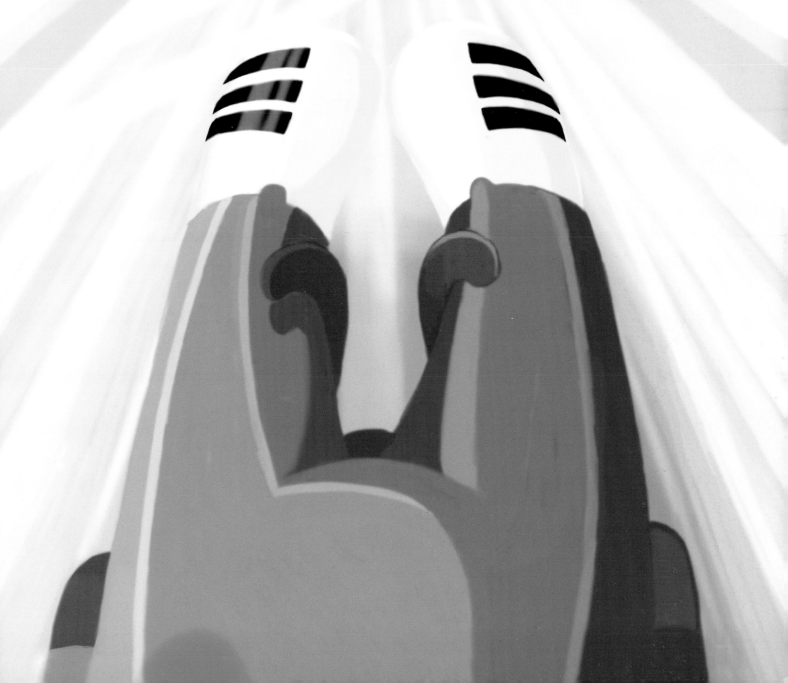

Her **legs** help her steer down the long, icy track.

Swish!

Down a straightaway!

Swoosh!

'Round a curve!

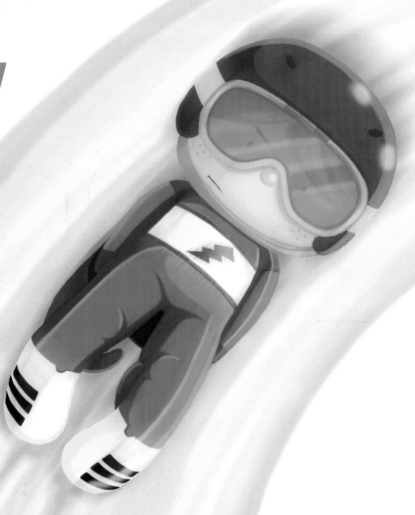

Lucy picks up speed

as she tries not to **swerve.**

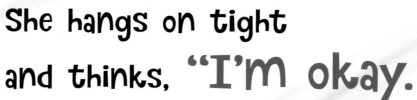

She hangs on tight
and thinks, "I'm okay.

This is just like tobogganing
at home on my sleigh."

Lucy stays lying flat,
just her head raised to see
the next bend up ahead...

And ZOOM–
through with ease!

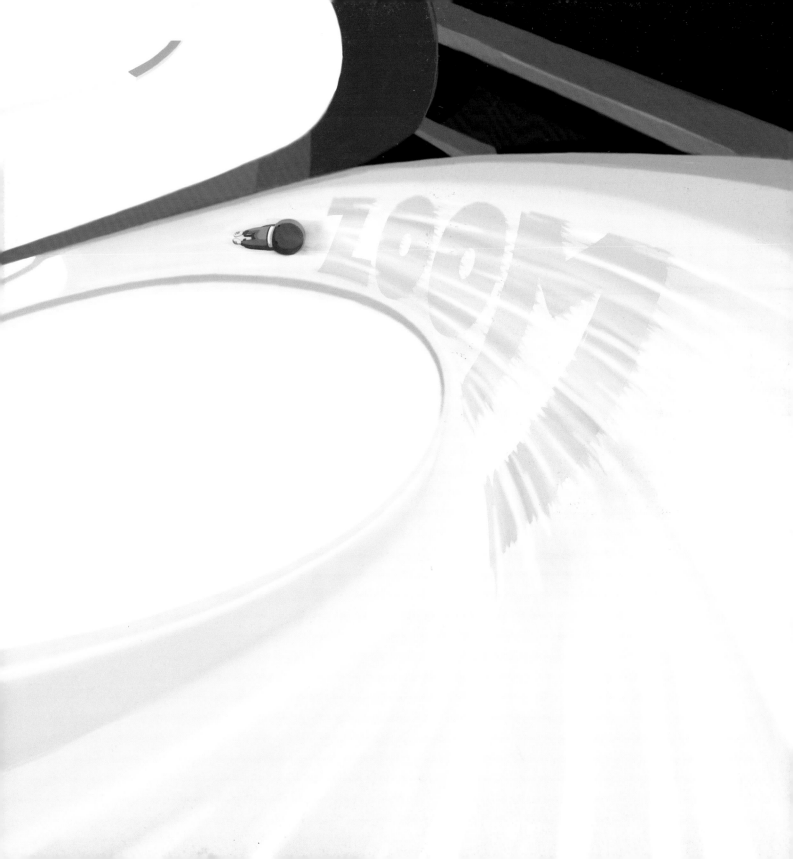

Lucy finds a good line.

Oh my!
What a thrill!

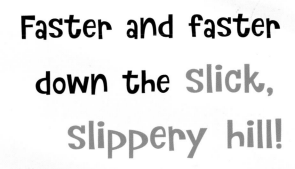

Faster and faster
down the slick,
slippery hill!

And then in a flash
she crosses the line!
Lucy looks at the clock
and sees her quick time.

Her parents both cheer
as she slows the sled down.
"Way to go! What a ride!
You make us so proud!"

"Hooray!" Lucy shouts.
"That ride felt too short.
It's fun to go fast!
What a cool
winter sport!"

FAST FACTS!

What does luge mean?
Luge is the French word for sled.

Where did it start?
The first luge race was held in St. Moritz, Switzerland, in the 1880s. It's an old sport!

How fast can top racers go?

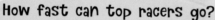

Manuel Pfister of Austria reached a top speed of 154 kilometers per hour (96 miles per hour) on the track in Whistler, British Columbia. That's faster than a car on the highway!

Why do sliders wear a speed suit?
Luge race suits are custom-made using high-tech fabrics. They fit tightly, like a second skin, so there is little wind resistance to slow racers down.

How do sliders steer?
They steer by applying pressure on the runners (also called *kufens*), the two candy-cane-shaped bows at the end of the sled. Using their legs, sliders push on the left runner to go right and on the right runner to go left.

For Rachel.
—L.B.

For Paula.
—J.H.

Text copyright © 2015 Lisa Bowes
Illustrations copyright © 2015 James Hearne

Library and Archives Canada Cataloguing in Publication

Bowes, Lisa, 1966–, author
Lucy tries luge / Lisa Bowes ; illustrated by James Hearne.
(Lucy tries sports)

Originally published: [Calgary, Alberta] : Bowes Knows Sports, © 2013.

ISBN 978-1-4598-1019-8 (pbk.).—ISBN 978-1-4598-1020-4 (pdf).—
ISBN 978-1-4598-1021-1 (epub)

I. Hearne, James, 1972–, illustrator II. Title.
PS8603.09758L83 2015   jc813'.6   C2015-901556-1
C2015-901557-X

First published in the United States, 2015
Library of Congress Control Number: 2015934242

Summary: Lucy overcomes her fears and learns to love luge, a winter sliding sport.

MIX
Paper from responsible sources
FSC® C016245

Orca Book Publishers is dedicated to preserving the environment and has printed this book on Forest Stewardship Council® certified paper.

Orca Book Publishers gratefully acknowledges the support for its publishing programs provided by the following agencies: the Government of Canada through the Canada Book Fund and the Canada Council for the Arts, and the Province of British Columbia through the BC Arts Council and the Book Publishing Tax Credit.

Artwork created using hand drawings and digital coloring.

Cover artwork by James Hearne
Design by Teresa Bubela

ORCA BOOK PUBLISHERS
www.orcabook.com

Printed and bound in Canada.

18 17 16 15 • 4 3 2 1